EARLY BIRD
STORIES

STRICTLY
NO CROCS

Early★Reader

First American edition published in 2019 by Lerner Publishing Group, Inc.

An original concept by Heather Pindar
Copyright © 2019 Heather Pindar

Illustrated by Susan Batori

First published by Maverick Arts Publishing Limited

Maverick
arts publishing

Licensed Edition
Strickly No Crocs

Lerner Publications Company
A division of Lerner Publishing Group, Inc.
241 First Avenue North
Minneapolis, MN 55401 USA

For reading levels and more information, look up this title at
www.lernerbooks.com.

Main body text set in Mikado a. Typeface provided by HVD Fonts.

Library of Congress Cataloging-in-Publication Data

Names: Pindar, Heather, author. | Batori, Susan, illustrator.
Title: Strictly no crocs / by Heather Pindar ; illustrated by Susan Batori.
Description: First American edition. | Minneapolis : Lerner Publications, 2019. |
    Series: Early bird readers. Blue (Early bird stories).
Identifiers: LCCN 2018018059 (print) | LCCN 2018027520 (ebook) |
    ISBN 9781541543317 (eb pdf) | ISBN 9781541541764 (lb : alk. paper) |
    ISBN 9781541546189 (pb : alk. paper)
Subjects: LCSH: Readers—Parties. | Readers—Animals. | Readers (Primary) |
    Parties—Juvenile literature. | Animals—Juvenile literature.
Classification: LCC PE1127.P37 (ebook) | LCC PE1127.P37 P56 2019 (print) |
    DDC 428.6/2—dc23

LC record available at https://lccn.loc.gov/2018018059

Manufactured in the United States of America
1-45350-39000-8/2/2018

EARLY BIRD STORIES

STRICTLY NO CROCS

Heather Pindar

Illustrated by **Susan Batori**

Lerner Publications ◆ Minneapolis

Zebra was having a party.

She asked everyone to come, but . . .

. . . the crocs were not invited.

But the crocs wanted to go to the party.

"We can eat everyone up!" said Cruncher.

"But how will we get in?" said Chomper.

"We can dress up!" said Snapper.

"No one will spot us!"

So the crocs went to the party.

First Cruncher, then Chomper, and then Snapper.

They had a lot of fun!

Cruncher went on the bouncy castle.

Chomper played a game . . .

. . . and he won a bear!

Then everyone sang

"Happy Birthday To You!"

Zebra had a big cake.

Snapper ate too much!

Next it was time to dance.

The crocs sang:

"Na na na na na na na!"

Everyone had fun
popping balloons.

Bang!

Bang!

Then everyone went outside.

Ooooooohhhhhhh!

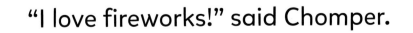

"I love fireworks!" said Chomper.

Soon the party was over.

Cruncher, Chomper, and Snapper said,

"Thank you!" and waved goodbye.

The crocs walked home.

"That was a great party!" said Chomper.

"Fantastic!" said Cruncher.

"Oh no!" said Snapper,

"We forgot to eat

everyone up!"

"Never mind," said Cruncher.

"It's Giraffe's birthday party
next week . . ."

Quiz

1. What animals are not invited to Zebra's birthday party?
   a) Crocodiles
   b) Giraffes
   c) Lions

2. What does Cruncher bounce on?
   a) A bed
   b) A bouncy castle
   c) A trampoline

3. What does everyone do to the balloons?
   a) Pop them
   b) Throw them
   c) Sit on them

4. Whose party is it next week?
   a) Lion's
   b) Giraffe's
   c) Monkey's

5. What do the Crocs forget to do?
   a) Sing "Happy Birthday"
   b) Say "thank you"
   c) Eat everybody up

EARLY BIRD
ST⊘RIES

Leveled for Guided Reading

Early Bird Stories have been edited and leveled by leading educational consultants to correspond with guided reading levels. The levels are assigned by taking into account the content, language style, layout, and phonics used in each book.

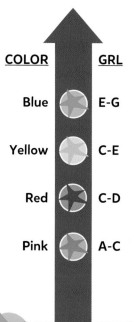

COLOR	GRL
Blue	E-G
Yellow	C-E
Red	C-D
Pink	A-C